THE ADVENTURES OF
RUBY AND WINK
THE BEGINNING

AMY KURTH

DEDICATED TO

FOR LINCOLN, JORDY, WYATT, CODY, BROOKS, HERA AND COLE.

IN HONOR OF SHIRLEY WHO READ TO ME DAILY AND BEULAH WHOSE WRITINGS STIRRED MY SOUL. BOTH CONTINUE TO INSPIRE ME DAILY.

A PORTION OF THE PROCEEDS OF THIS BOOK WILL BE DONATED TO ANIMAL RESCUE ORGANIZATIONS

SOMETIMES THINGS HAPPEN AND PETS HAVE TO LEAVE, AND BOTH FAMILIES AND PETS ARE SADDENED AND GRIEVE.

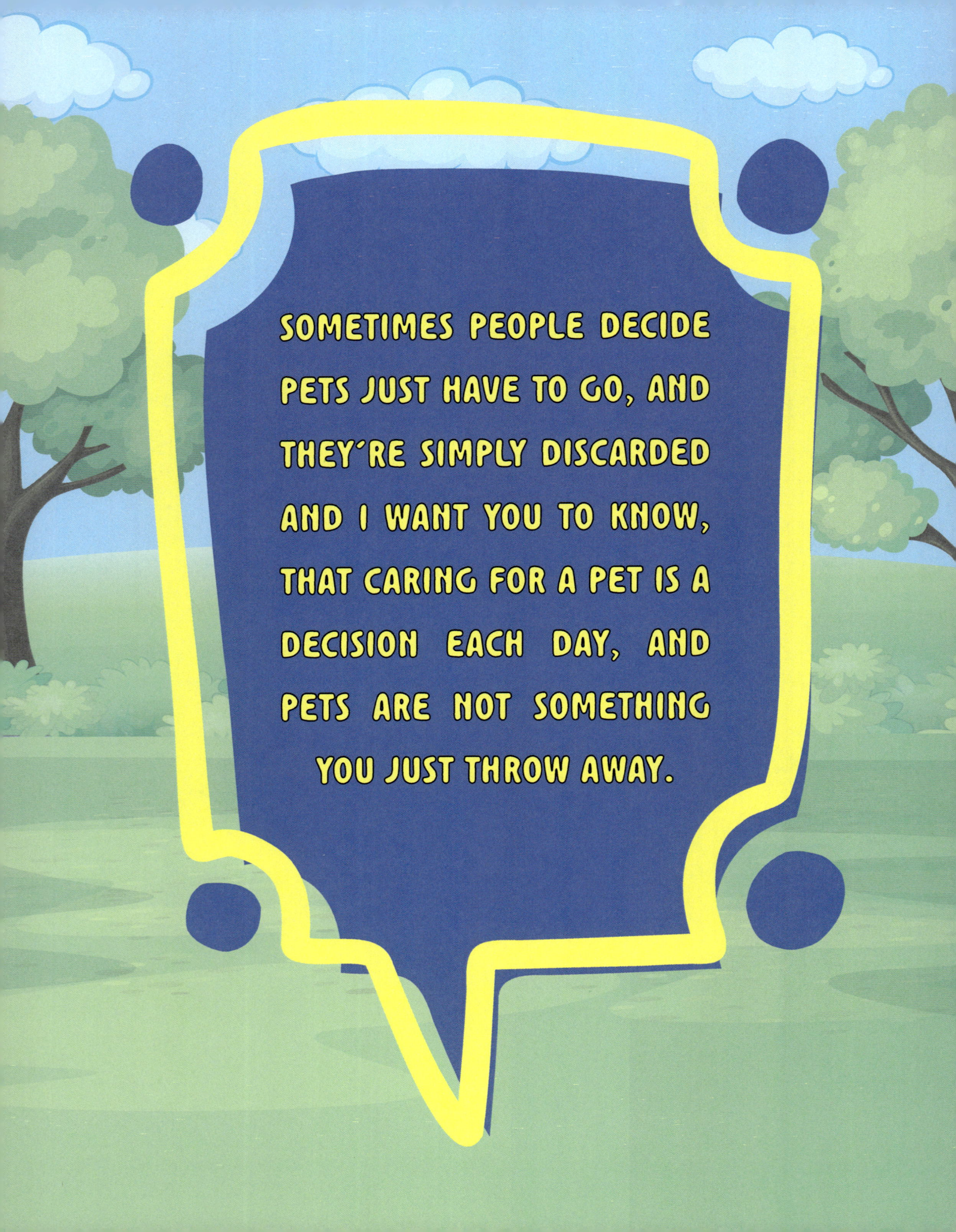

SOMETIMES PEOPLE DECIDE PETS JUST HAVE TO GO, AND THEY'RE SIMPLY DISCARDED AND I WANT YOU TO KNOW, THAT CARING FOR A PET IS A DECISION EACH DAY, AND PETS ARE NOT SOMETHING YOU JUST THROW AWAY.

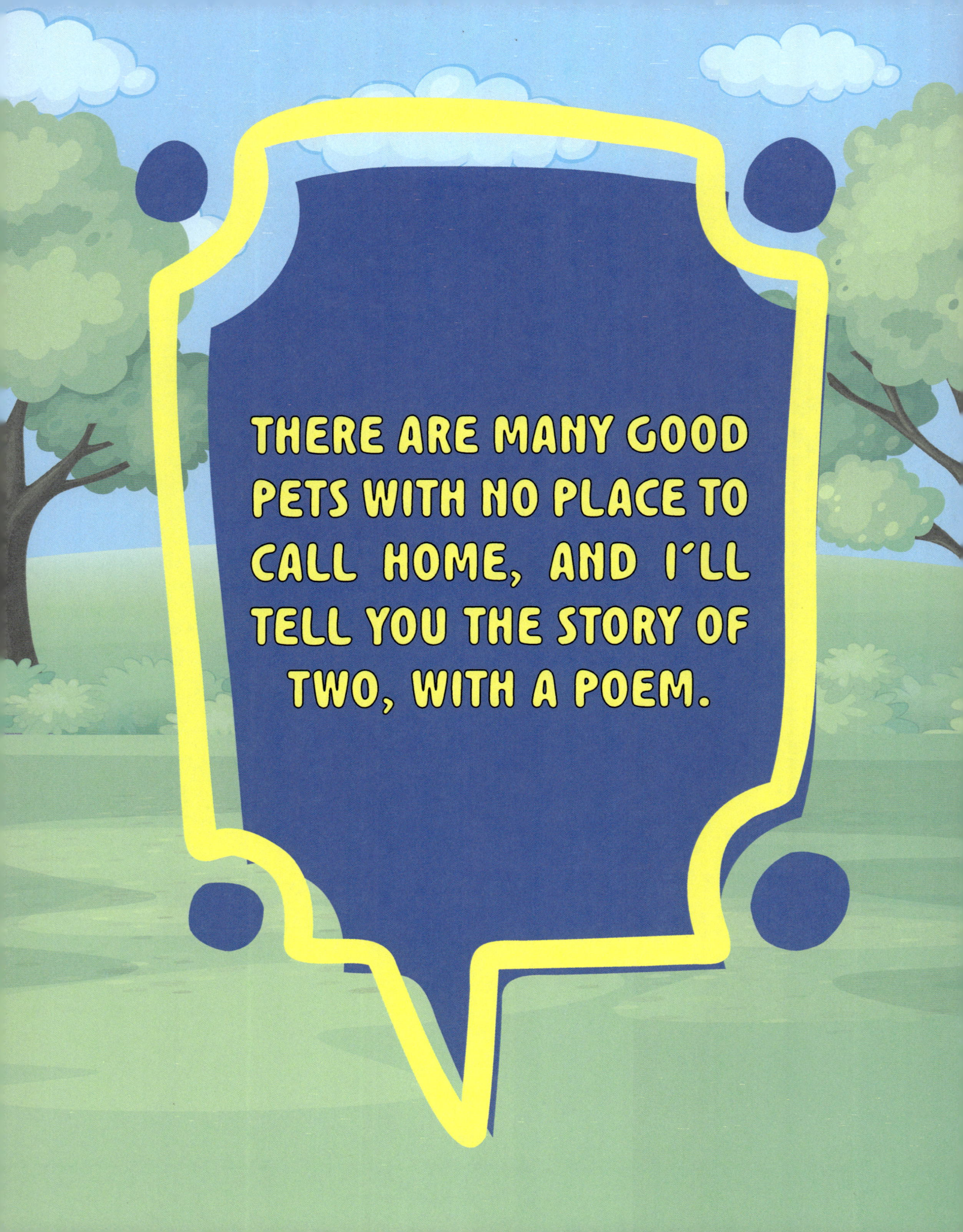

THERE ARE MANY GOOD PETS WITH NO PLACE TO CALL HOME, AND I'LL TELL YOU THE STORY OF TWO, WITH A POEM.

CUDDLY AND CUTE, AND FOREVER LOVED YOU WOULD THINK, BUT THAT IS NOT THE STORY OF RUBY AND WINK.

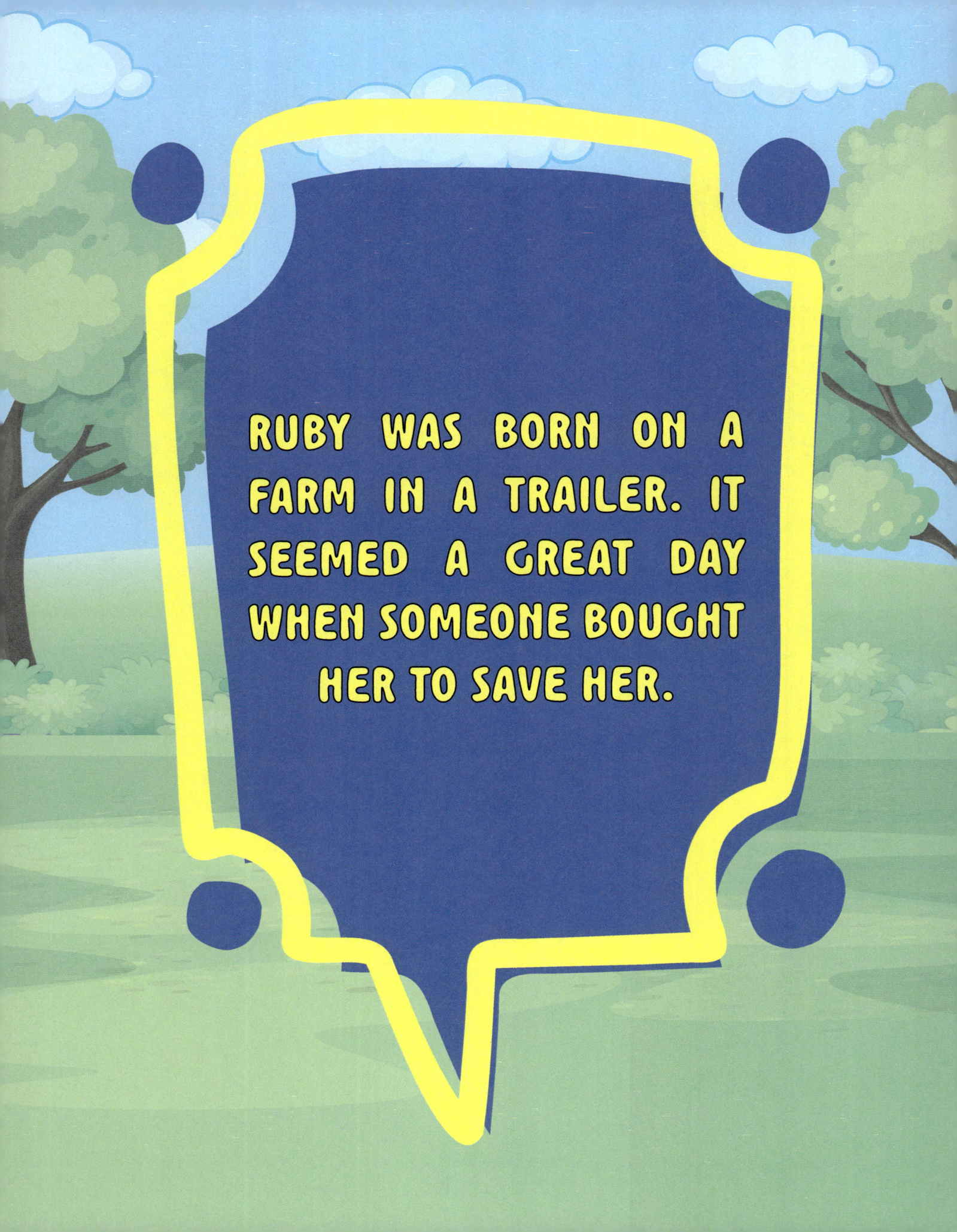

RUBY WAS BORN ON A FARM IN A TRAILER. IT SEEMED A GREAT DAY WHEN SOMEONE BOUGHT HER TO SAVE HER.

BUT PUPPIES ARE NOT EASY, AND BEFORE SHE WAS ONE SHE WAS OUT OF HER HOME, RUBY'S OWNER WAS DONE.

WINK WAS OWNED BY A BREEDER FOR YEARS. SHE HAD PUPPIES AND PUPPIES WITH LONG FLOPPY EARS.

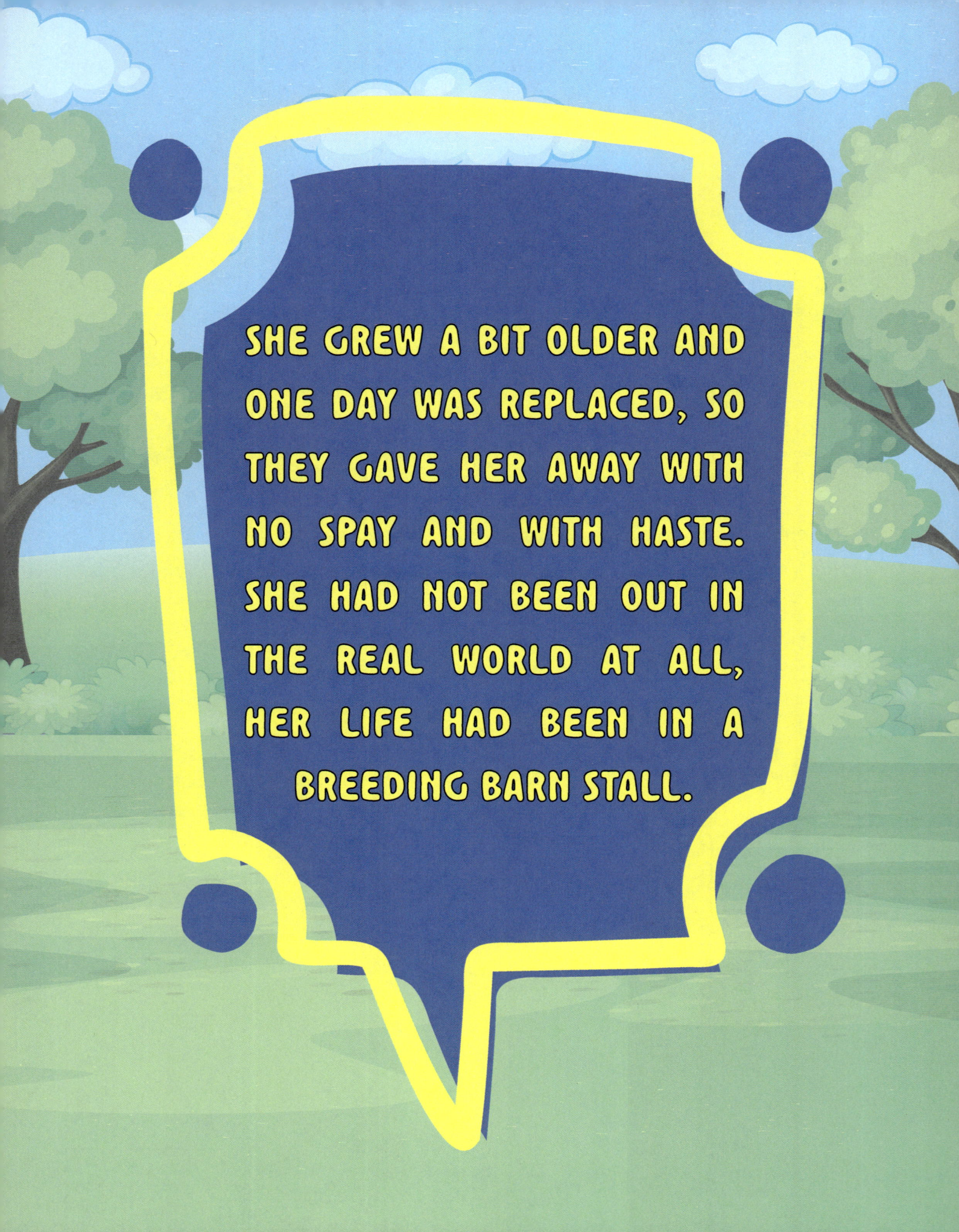

SHE GREW A BIT OLDER AND ONE DAY WAS REPLACED, SO THEY GAVE HER AWAY WITH NO SPAY AND WITH HASTE. SHE HAD NOT BEEN OUT IN THE REAL WORLD AT ALL, HER LIFE HAD BEEN IN A BREEDING BARN STALL.

RUBY KNEW PEOPLE THAT HELPED GIRLS LIKE HER OUT, SO SHE CAME HERE TO LIVE, SHE'D BE HAPPY, NO DOUBT. SHE'D BE WARM AND FED AND TAUGHT SOME NEW THINGS. SHE'D DEVELOP SOME CONFIDENCE AND STRETCH HER NEW WINGS.

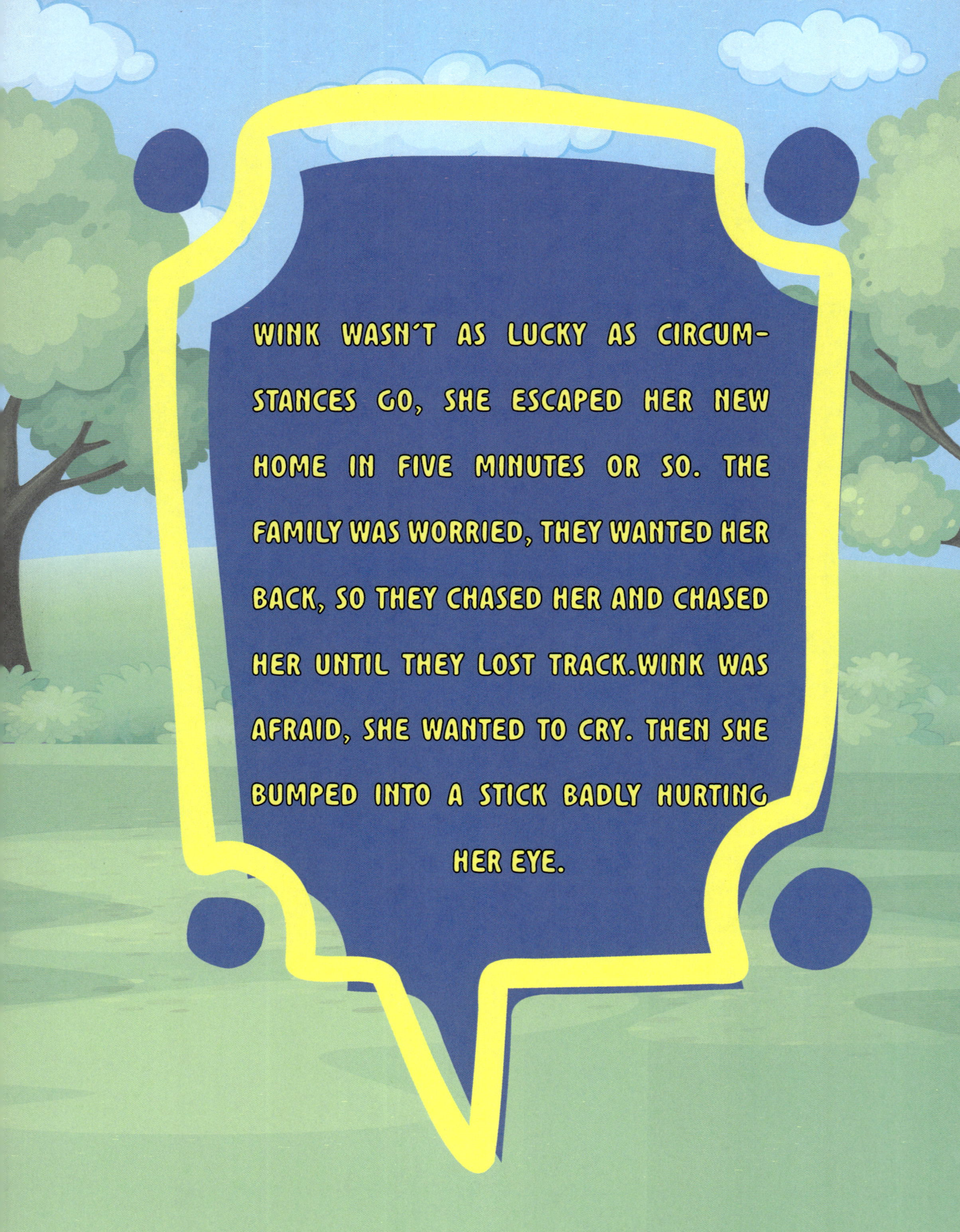

WINK WASN'T AS LUCKY AS CIRCUM-
STANCES GO, SHE ESCAPED HER NEW
HOME IN FIVE MINUTES OR SO. THE
FAMILY WAS WORRIED, THEY WANTED HER
BACK, SO THEY CHASED HER AND CHASED
HER UNTIL THEY LOST TRACK.WINK WAS
AFRAID, SHE WANTED TO CRY. THEN SHE
BUMPED INTO A STICK BADLY HURTING
HER EYE.

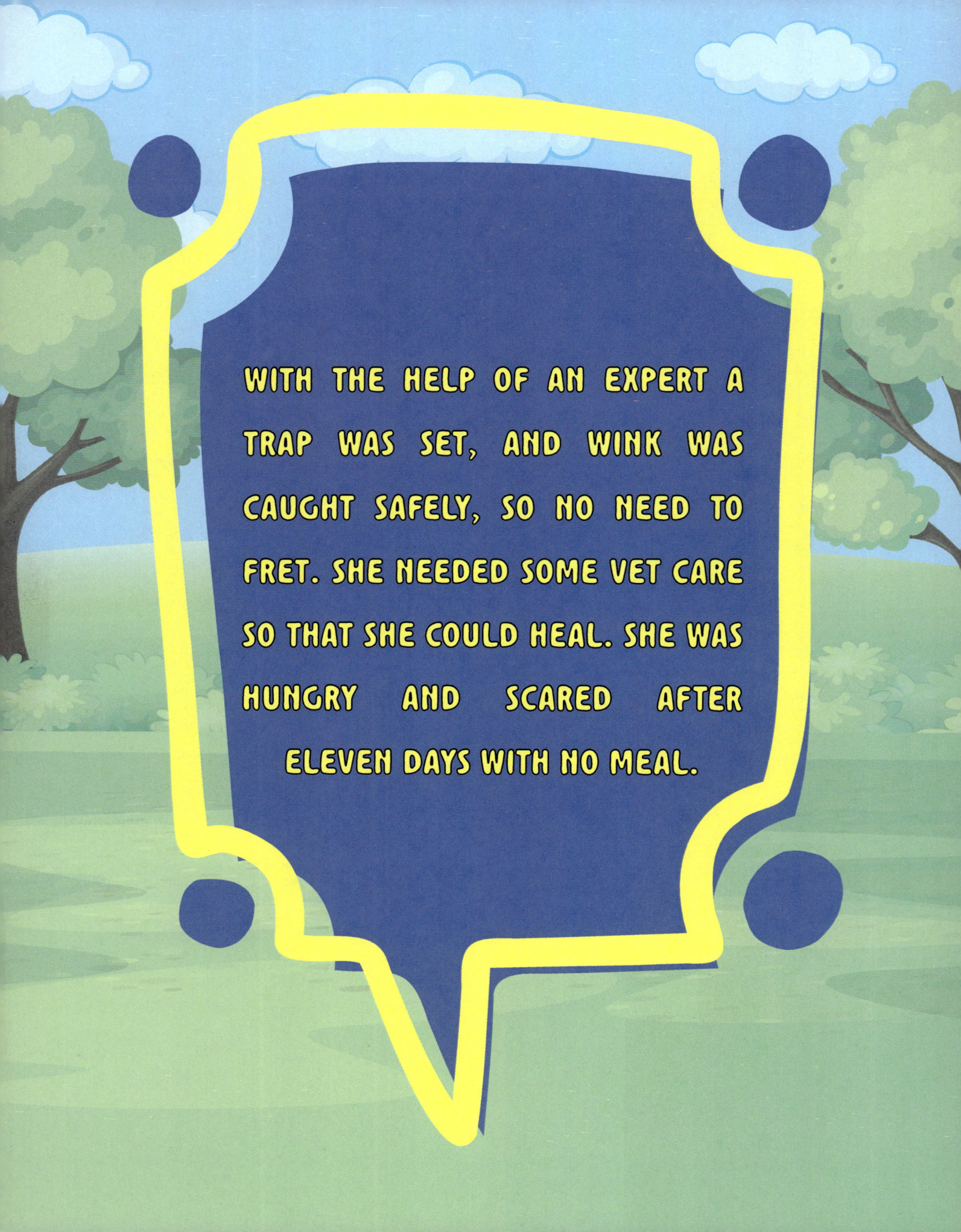

WITH THE HELP OF AN EXPERT A TRAP WAS SET, AND WINK WAS CAUGHT SAFELY, SO NO NEED TO FRET. SHE NEEDED SOME VET CARE SO THAT SHE COULD HEAL. SHE WAS HUNGRY AND SCARED AFTER ELEVEN DAYS WITH NO MEAL.

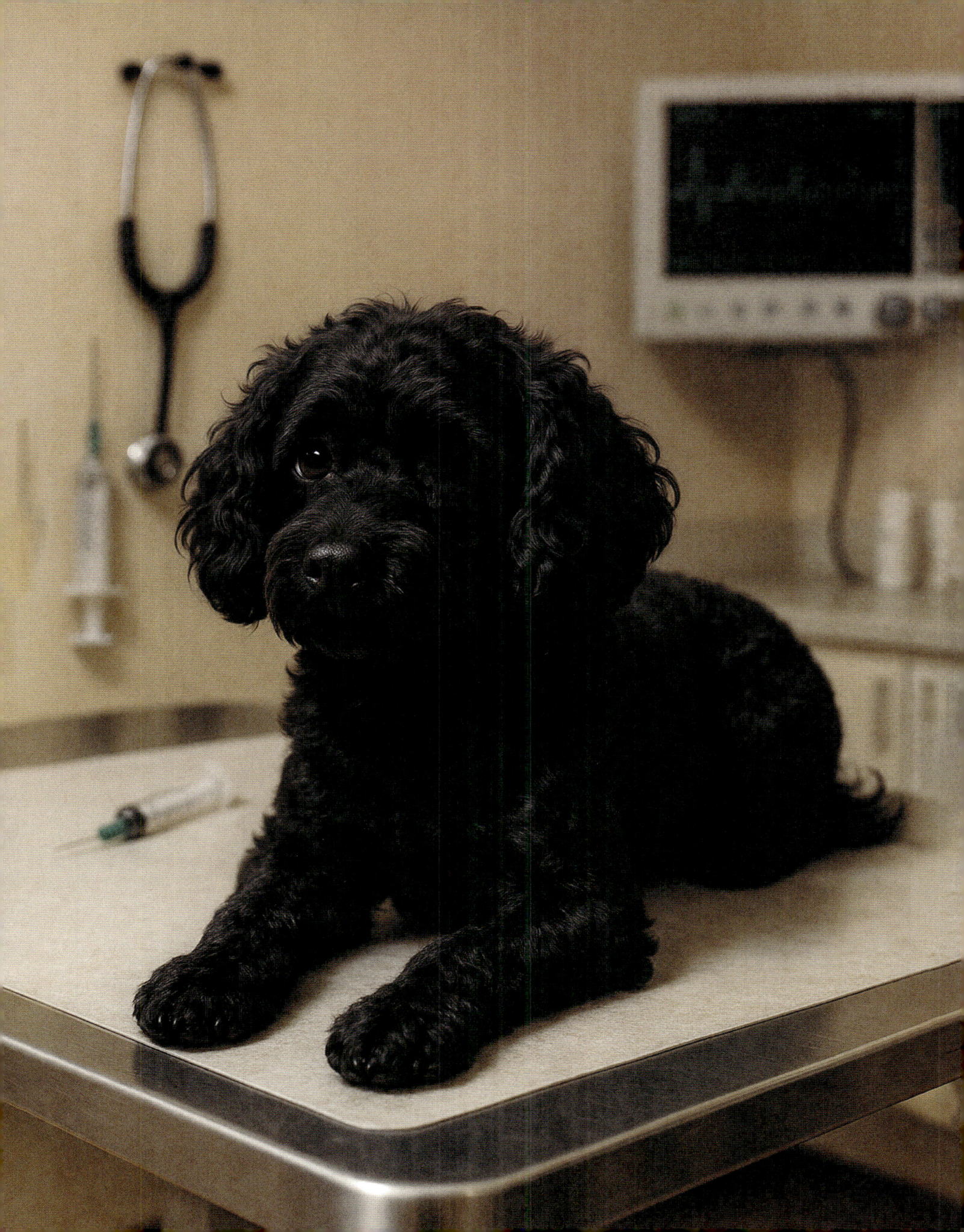

WINK CAME TO STAY WHERE RUBY HAD

LANDED, AND BOTH BEGAN LEARNING TO TAKE

LOVING FOR GRANTED. THEY HAD WARM BEDS AND FOOD

AND PLAY TIME OUTSIDE. THAT IS SOMETHING DOGS NEED THAT

GOOD OWNERS PROVIDE. THEY STARTED OUT SLOWLY NOT SURE

HOW TO FEEL, FINDING COMFORT TOGETHER THEIR FRIENDSHIP

WAS REAL. AS THE WEEKS PASSED THEY BLOSSOMED AND GREW,

FINDING THEMSELVES HERE SEEMED TOO GOOD TO BE TRUE.

RUBY AND WINK ADVENTURE EACH DAY, NEVER AGAIN WON-

DERING WHERE IT IS THEY WILL STAY. THIS IS JUST THE BEGIN-

NING IT ISN´T THE END, HAPPY TOGETHER, FOREVER

BEST FRIENDS.THAT IS THEIR STORY TOLD WITH

A POEM. RUBY AND WINK ARE FOREVER

NOW HOME.